RUDE FOOD

Photographed by David Thorpe.
Written by Pierre Le Poste. Designed by Martin Reavley.

BALLANTINE BOOKS · NEW YORK

Published in the United States by Ballantine Books, a division of Random House, Inc. New York.

Previously published in Great Britain by Aurum Press Limited in 1978 and by Macmillan London Limited in 1981.

Library of Congress Catalog Card Number: 79-52260

ISBN 0-345-31234-1

Typography by Olaf Luinberg & Phil Lev
Styling by Barbara Drake. Food by Beryl Cartier

Manufactured in the United States of America

First American Edition: February 1980
Second Printing: August 1983

10 9 8 7 6 5 4 3 2 1

INTRODUCTION

The association between food and sex has been firmly established ever since that old business with Adam, Eve and the apple.

This book is merely a reminder of the added pleasures that can be derived from simple food when it is imaginatively chosen, presented and eaten.

All you need are the ingredients and a dirty mind.

Bon Appetit!

THE COCKTAIL AND OTHER APERITIFS.

America took the Dry Martini firmly to its bosom many years ago, and it is still by far the most popular cocktail.

Controversies have raged over such vital matters as the proportion of vermouth to gin, pitted versus unpitted olives and other aspects of the ritual.

The best Martinis we ever had were made by a fanatic who maintained a separate icebox in which he kept everything necessary for his passion.

The gin was chilled, the vermouth was chilled, the glasses were chilled — even the olives were chilled. This, he said, was the secret of the perfect Martini.

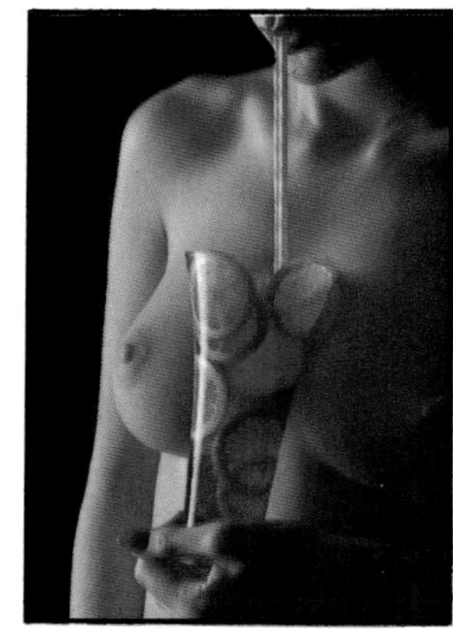

After two large ones, we were in no state to disagree with him. After three large ones, we would have followed him anywhere.

In fact, the Martini is far too potent to be called an aperitif.

It is much better suited to people seeking oblivion than those in search of a good dinner.

The true aperitif usually looks

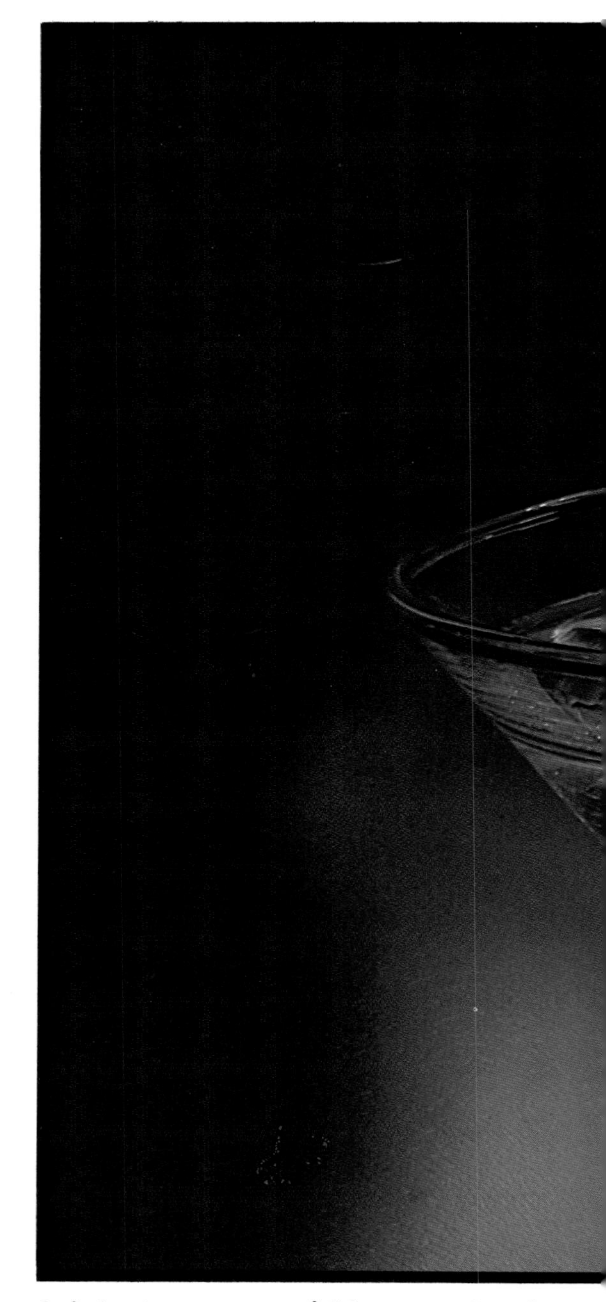

fairly tame; you'd be pushed to s anything erotic in a glass of she

However, there's nothing t stop you inventing your own m colourful concoctions, as we ha

There are no rules except this one: don't make the drinks strong, otherwise the evening may end in the bathroom instea of the bedroom.

FOOD FOR FOREPLAY.

The first course in a meal of rude food should perform the same function as a hand on the thigh: it should alert the senses for the joys that are to come.

It's best to avoid heavy or complicated dishes.

One of the rudest chefs we know never serves a first course that requires the use of both hands; he feels that you should be able to eat *and* toy with your partner at the same time.

Whether that's strictly necessary or not is a matter of personal choice, but you should try to keep away from any dish that is too demanding of your attention. The purpose of this meal, after all, is not merely to eat.

As you will see from the suggestions that follow, we are great believers in letting nature do the work, rather than the cook.

First-class ingredients, left in their natural state as much as possible, are always light on the palate and easy on the eye.

THE PERFECT START.

Long, moist, tender and faintly embarrassing, nothing can beat asparagus as the first course in an evening of rude food.

Be warned, however. It has to be really good asparagus, carefully prepared, otherwise it tends to be stringy and unromantic.

All but the smallest shoots need peeling (if you don't have the special gadget, a potato peeler will do fine) before going into a pan of boiling, salted water for 5 to 10 minutes, depending on the thickness.

Eat it warm or cold, with melted butter or a Hollandaise sauce.

Knives and forks are not allowed; asparagus must be eaten with the fingers.

There are several other classic starters which we like very much because they are served raw.

This makes them somehow naughtier than cooked starters, and it obviously cuts down on time spent in the kitchen.

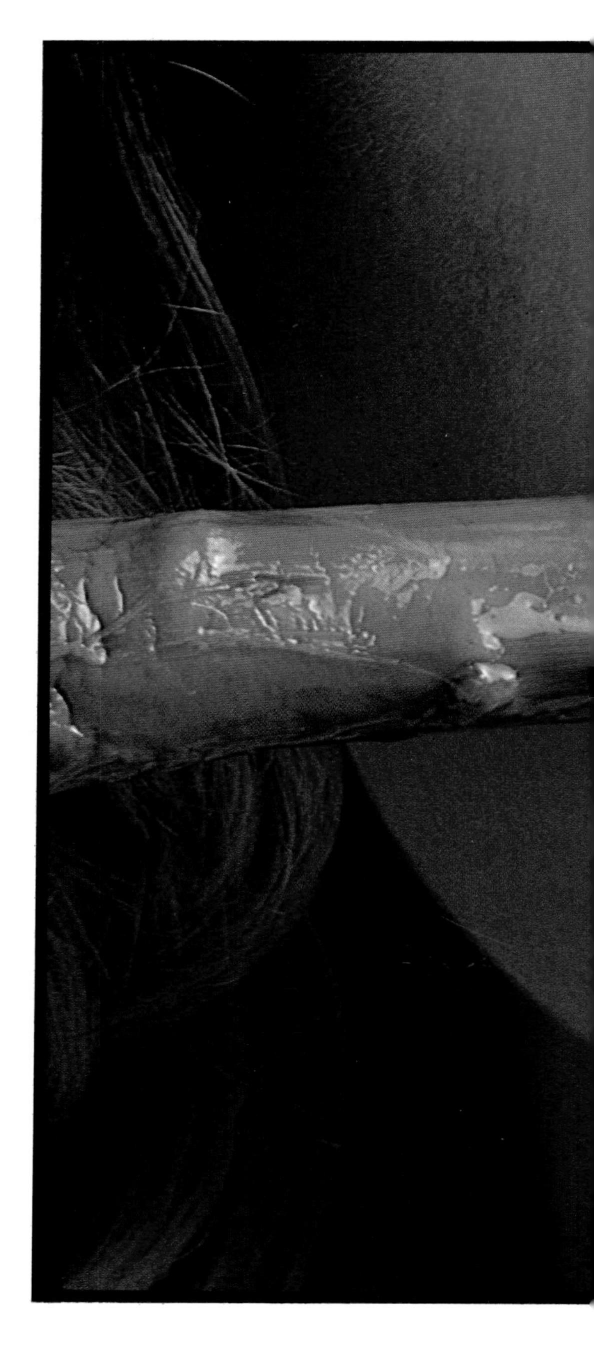

LES CRUDITES.

These are the raw, crisp elements of an hors d'oeuvre.

If you can't find really good fresh vegetables, don't bother.

Raw food must be perfect.

Can be served on their own or with a 'dip'.

ARTICHOKES.

You don't just eat artichokes; you undress them.

Hence their popularity in rude menus.

To cook, boil them in salted water until a leaf can be pulled out easily.

Drain well and serve hot with melted butter to dip the leaves into, or cold with an Hollandaise sauce.

OYSTERS.

Someone once said that eating a good oyster feels like angels copulating on your tongue.

Even this sublime experience is better with a bottle of Sancerre.

They should be opened just before eating and served with quarters of lemon and brown bread and butter.

CAVIAR.

Worth saving up for, the best caviar is generally eaten as is, au naturel, on a piece of thin freshly made toast.

Lesser grades can be served sprinkled with finely chopped onion or grated yolks of hard-boiled eggs.

FRENCH DRESSING.

Unlike factory prepared salad dressings, which taste like liquid gunpowder, a true French dressing is delicate and subtle.

It is one of the easiest things of all to make, providing you have excellent ingredients.

You must have superb olive oil and a genuine white or red wine vinegar.

Use four parts of oil to one of vinegar. Pour directly on to the salad. Mix with your hands until every leaf is coated with a thin film of dressing. Add a dusting of black pepper.

If you have made the dressing correctly, you will see your partner's lips become slightly oily as the salad is consumed.

The best olive oil comes from Lucca, Italy. Ask for *first* pressing, which tastes as good as it sounds.

THE MAIN COURSE.

In this part of the meal, it is not easy to be rude unless you are a reasonably accomplished cook.

The preparation of sauces, garnishes and other gastro-erotic aids requires skill as well as imagination.

We've included one complicated dish – Sole Colbert – because it is a classic.

However, our other suggestions are not too difficult to prepare. If they inspire you to experiment, remember that true rudeness comes from the shape and texture of the ingredients.

As a general rule, the less you need to do to them the better.

SOLE COLBERT.

It takes quite an accomplished cook to prepare what has been called the most erotic fish dish of all.

The ingredients are nothing special – a skinned sole, some small shrimp, plenty of parsley and a cream sauce.

The trick is to arrange everything so that the soft white fillets curve gently round the creamy sauce rather like two long lips.

Surround them with thick curls of parsley, insert the shrimp, and the effect is – well, you get the idea.

Incidentally, fish is supposed to be good for the brain as well as the libido.

CIVILISED RAW MEAT.

For a dish that consists almost entirely of ground beef, steak tartare has an impressive reputation.

According to popular legend, it does wonders for your sex life – something that has never been claimed for the humble hamburger.

Another part of the mystique is the story of how steak tartare got its name.

The whole thing was started, so we're told, by the tartar horsemen of Genghis Khan.

They developed the unsanitary habit of keeping their meat under the saddle, and riding on it until it became tender enough to eat without cooking.

The flavour left a little to be desired, but the texture was sublime.

Fortunately, the butcher has now replaced the bum, and you can buy ground fillet steak that needs very little work from you before it becomes a meal.

Here's the basic recipe, which you can easily adapt to make the taste more or less 'hot'.

Blend a raw egg into the ground fillet steak. Add tabasco, salt and coarse milled black pepper to taste. Serve with thin fresh toast in a napkin.

STRICT PASTA.

Cooked properly, pasta has the perfect texture for a classic rude food dish – firm, plump and slightly slippery between the lips.

Unfortunately, it usually appears hidden beneath a dollop of meat or tomato-flavoured sauce which conceals the subtle taste of the pasta beneath.

Here is a recipe that requires no sauce to bring it to life; a dusting of black pepper and grated cheese is all you need.

Add the pasta to boiling salted water in a large pan.

The cooking time will vary according to the type of pasta.

Test between your teeth.

Drain well and serve with butter, pepper and grated parmesan.

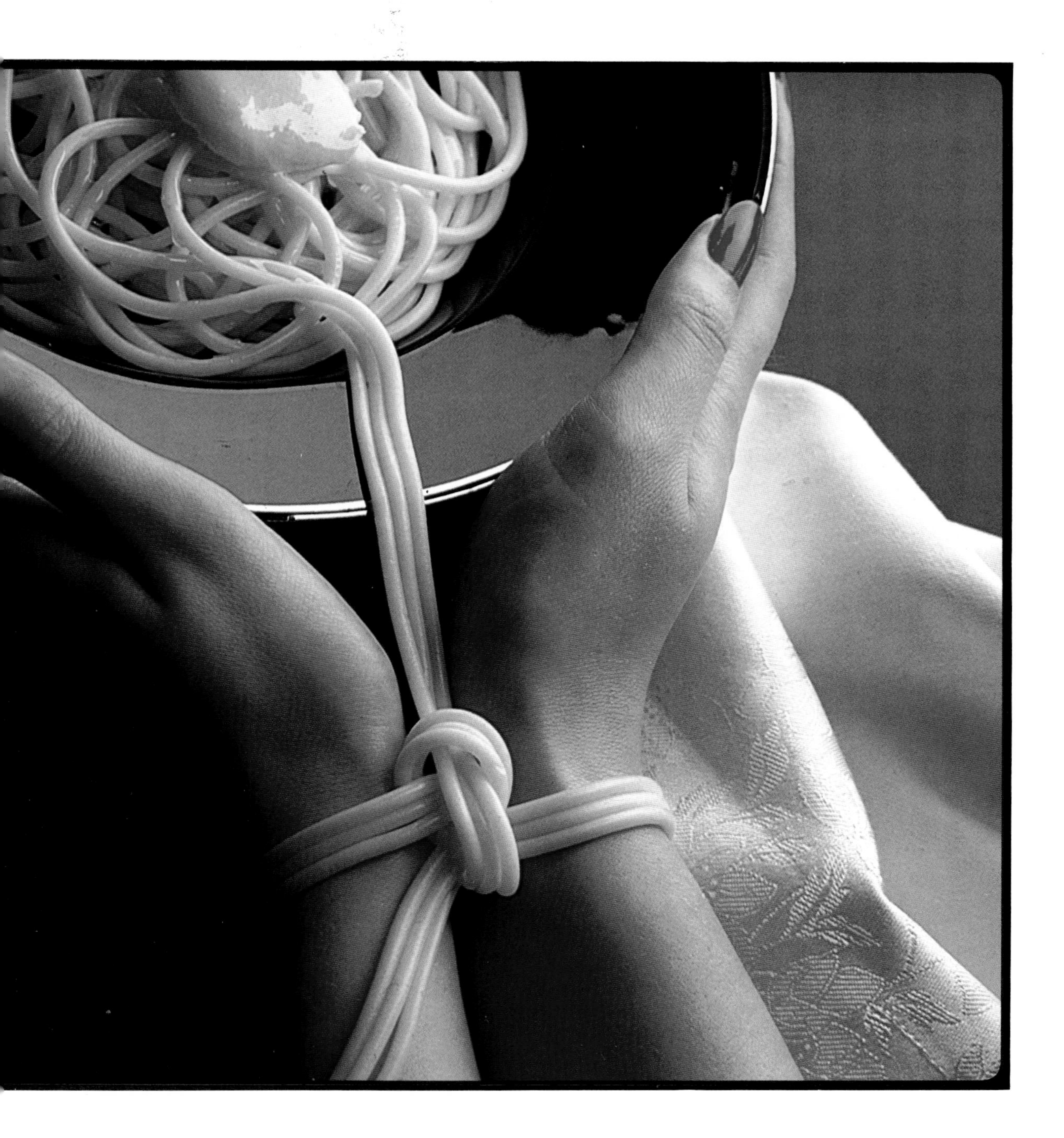

HOW TO DEVELOP YOUR MUSSELS.

This is our favourite recipe for moules marinières – the world's most sensuous soup.

First wash and scrub the mussels thoroughly under a running tap. Make sure they are free of sand, mud and beards.

Then put them in a large pan with a clove of garlic and a large glass of dry white wine to every quart of mussels.

Cook quickly until the mussels open.

Remove them and keep warm.

Strain the stock, reheat and pour over the mussels adding chopped parsley.

To wash it down, something clean and uncomplicated like Muscadet is perfect.

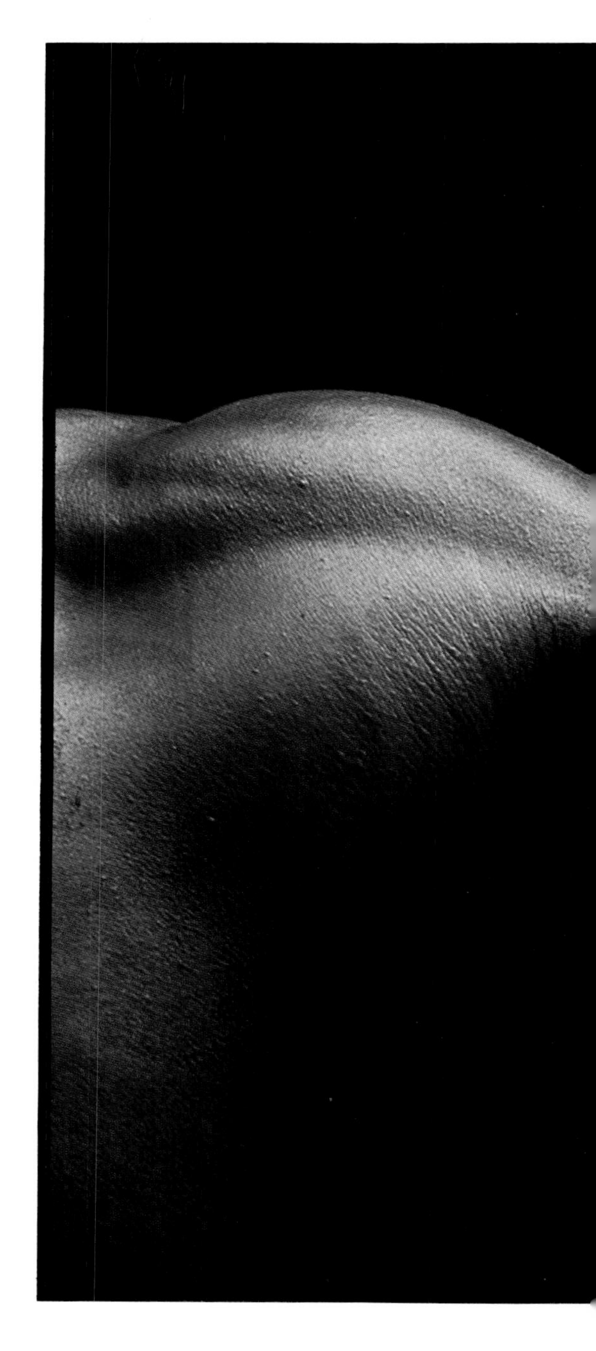

THE PEDIGREE HOT DOG

The best hot dogs bear little resemblance to those steaming horrors sold in cinema foyers.

For a great hot dog, you must start with a great frankfurter. Harrods has a good selection of the genuine, meat-filled article, canned in brine.

The difference in taste between these and the plastic-wrapped, bread-stuffed frankfurter found in supermarkets is vast.

Next, you need a large and fairly fierce onion, a fresh soft bun and some spicy (rather than explosively strong) mustard.

Chop the onion into rings and slide them on to the cooked frankfurter.

Spread mustard generously onto a warm bun, insert the frankfurter and serve to your beloved.

THE RUDEST COURSE OF ALL.

The dessert presents almost unlimited opportunities to anyone with a dirty mind.

The natural shapes of fruit, the heavy thickness of whipped cream, the rich and sinful consistency of chocolate—if you can't be rude at this stage of the meal, you'll never be rude at all.

On the following pages you will find one or two ideas that may intrigue you.

Most of them are very simple, but they do require the best possible raw ingredients.

One flawless peach is better than a basket of bruised fruit.

THE BANANA AND OTHER SPLITS.

A jaunty banana, two meringue halves, a well-aimed dollop of cream, and there you have a simple dessert with sex appeal.

Having mastered the split technique, you can use it with great effect elsewhere in the menu.

The asparagus split, with two grilled tomatoes in attendance, is guaranteed to break the ice at dinner parties.

And if you're on a budget, the frankfurter split (two scoops of mashed potato at one end and a dab of mustard on the other) is one way to beat the cost of meat.

Just follow the simple rule of two round, one long and you'll be able to do all kinds of splits.

Warning: Choose your guests carefully.

STRAWBERRIES IN ECSTASY.

The taste of fresh strawberries and thick cream is quite good enough for most people without any additions.

However, here are three delicious refinements which you may like to try.

Eton Mess is cream, a little sugar and chopped-up strawberries all mixed together in one voluptuous blob.

It tastes just as good as conventional strawberries and cream, but is not quite as photogenic.

Ivan's Weakness is strawberries marinated in chilled vodka for a few minutes before applying the cream.

The vodka doesn't fight with the flavour of the strawberries, but somehow accentuates it.

Darned ingenious, those Russians.

Strawberries Vinaigrette sound terrible, but in fact the contrast between the sweetness of the fruit and the sharpness of the dressing is sensational.

The tiny wild strawberries are best for this, but their larger relatives will do.

PEACHES BOTTOMS UP.

Skin your peaches, remove the stones and slice a little off each peach to make a flat base.

Cover the peaches with a light coating of the thinnest kind of honey, and serve with their little rumps uppermost.

(To liven up the honey sauce, you can always warm it gently and add brandy.)

THE ELEGANT WOBBLER.

Most people stop eating jellies after the age of six.

A great mistake. No other dessert can quite match the fleshy quiver of a firm and well-formed jelly.

Strategically placed cherries or grapes are optional.

If you're serving cream, there should be lots of it.

GROWN-UP SWEETS.

Petits fours look nice, but if you eat them at the end of the meal they completely ruin the taste of that last glass of wine.

We prefer to wait until about two in the morning, when we are often overtaken by the urge for a quick nibble.

Ideally, petits fours should be kept in a small refrigerator by the side of the bed, next to the champagne.

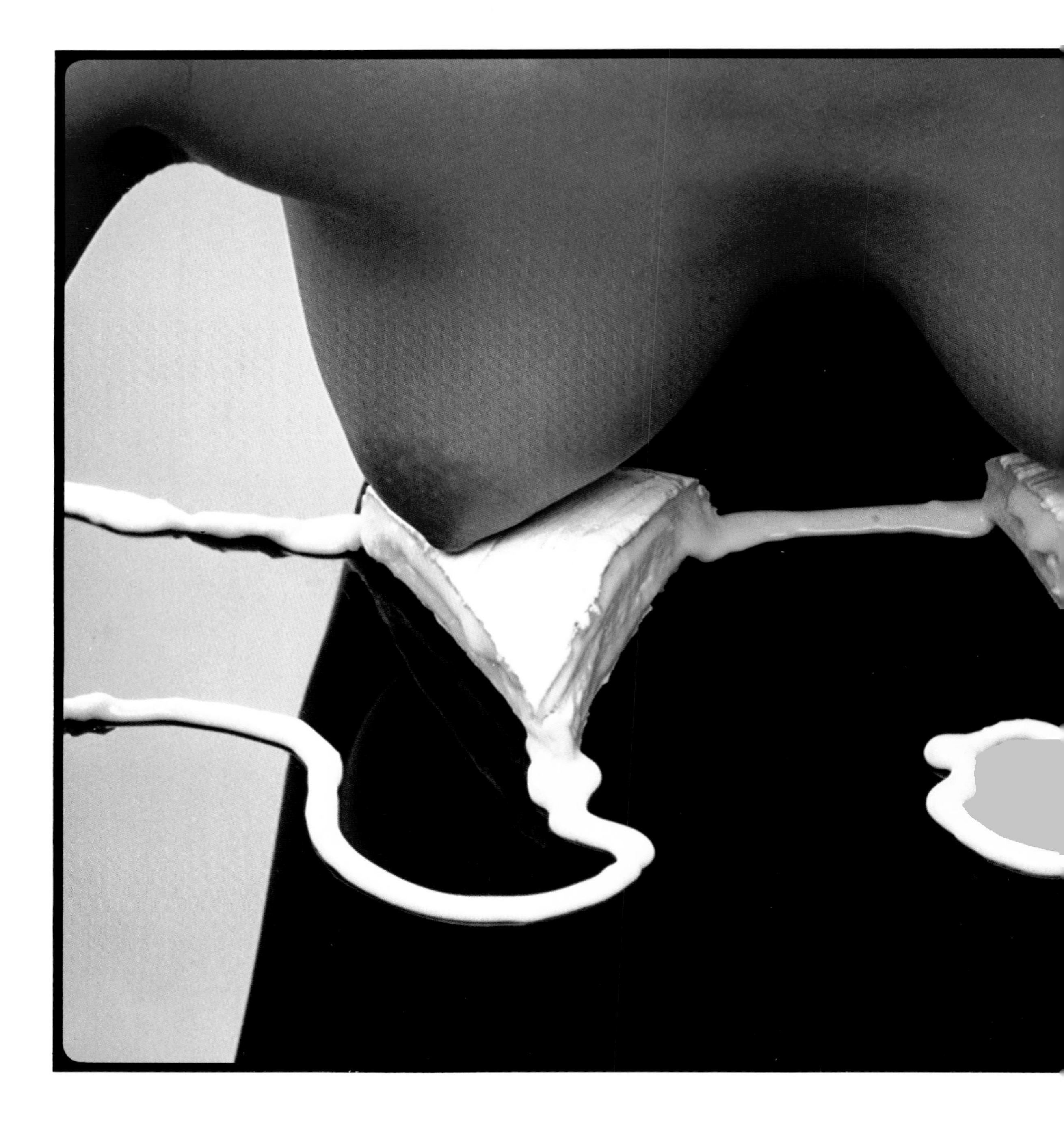

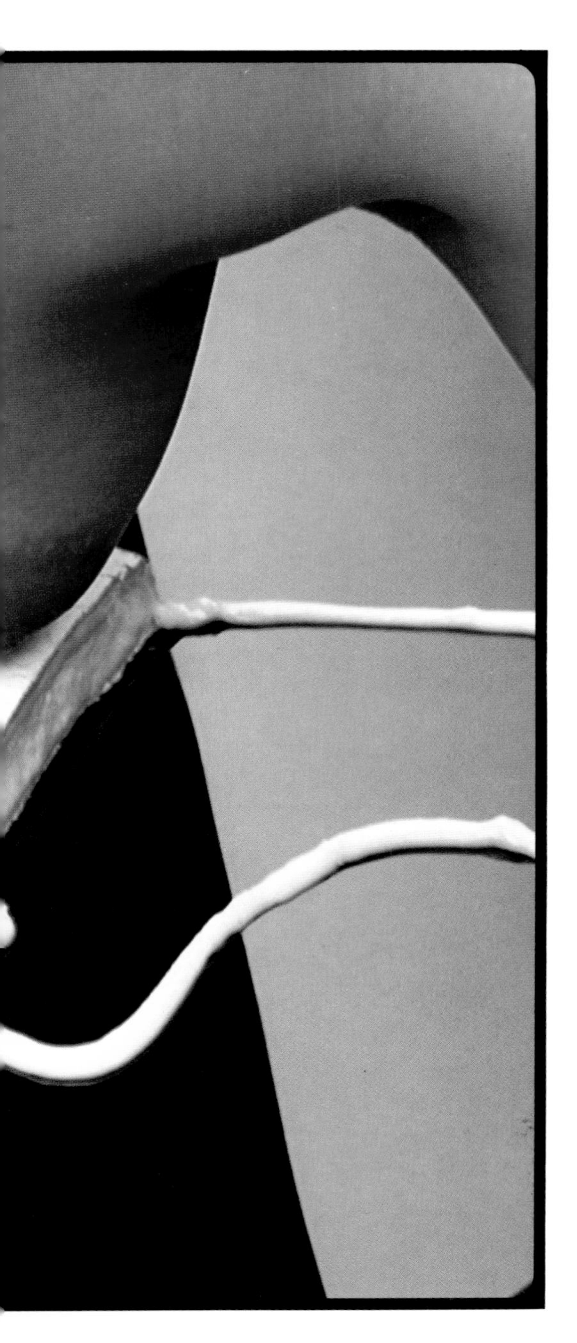

BRIE FOR TWO.

Of all the cheeses you could choose to end a meal of rude food, Brie is possibly the most sensuous.

A good piece – soft and ripe to the point of decadence – should practically sigh as you cut into it, and then ooze very, very slowly over the plate.

With Brie, timing is all.

Too young, and it will resemble one of those styrofoam wedges served in many restaurants.

Too old, and it will follow you round the room.

If there's a good cheese shop near you, ask the proprietor to give you a Brie that's ready for eating.

If there isn't a good cheese shop near you, stick to fruit.

NATURE'S LITTLE SNIFTER.

To hell with all those balloon glasses. Here is an infinitely more efficient and agreeable way of taking your after-dinner cognac.

The navel has two major advantages over the more conventional form of receptacle.

1. It is unbreakable.

2. It provides a constant, even warmth which brings out the bouquet of the cognac.

It is also a lot of fun.

DRESSING FOR THE KITCHEN.

Many great erotic cooks claim that they do their best work in the nude.

It is supposed to make them more nimble and alert, and to stimulate their creative juices.

If you ever feel tempted to follow their example, just remember that many a promising evening has been ruined by a few drops of sizzling oil landing on vital and unprotected parts.

Always wear an apron.

A good apron is thick, long and has plenty of storage space.

Those flimsy little numbers are only good for serving drinks.

There is no such thing as a sexy kitchen glove, so choose the most padded and utilitarian model you can find.